Buddy the Bluenose Reindeer

For Ben & Emmet

Merry Christmas

Love

Auntie Nancy

2001

Buddy the Bluenose Reindeer

Bruce Nunn

Illustrations by Brenda Jones

NIMBUS
PUBLISHING

Nimbus Publishing Limited
PO Box 9166
Halifax, NS   B3K 5M8
(902) 455-4286

Printed and bound in Canada

Author photo: Ryan Cameron, Northeast Magic; hair/makeup: Lisa Cail

Library and Archives Canada Cataloguing in Publication

> Nunn, Bruce, 1962-
> Buddy the bluenose reindeer /
> Bruce Nunn; illustrations by
> Brenda Jones.

> ISBN 1-55109-539-4

1. Christmas stories, Canadian (English). I. Jones, Brenda,
1953- II. Title.

PS8577.U5485B83 2005   jC813'.6   C2005-904353-9

The Canada Council | Le Conseil des Arts
for the Arts | du Canada

We acknowledge the financial support of the Government of Canada
through the Book Publishing Industry Development Program (BPIDP)
and the Canada Council, and of the Province of Nova Scotia through
the Department of Tourism, Culture and Heritage for our publishing
activities.

For all Nova Scotians,
at home and away.

ou know Santa's eight reindeer, don't you? Let's see…there are Dasher and Dancer, of course. And Prancer and Vixen…Oh! And who can forget Comet and Cupid and Donner—although some say "Donder"—and…ummmm…oh, yeah: Blitzen.

Everybody knows those names. And then of course there is reindeer number nine, Santa's most famous reindeer of all: Rudolph.

But we never hear about reindeer number ten. He was added to Santa's team of sleigh-pullers a long time ago, but he doesn't usually fly with the others. You see, reindeer number ten is an extra. He's a reindeer replacement. A backup buck, you might say.

Now, I'm not talking about Olive. This isn't "Olive, the other reindeer." That's just the kids' joke about the song. No, this special reindeer is a little four-legged fellow who grew up in the woods on the South Shore of Nova Scotia. Just wait till you hear. This Nova Scotian reindeer can ALSO guide Santa's sleigh at night because he too has a brightly illuminated proboscis!

What does that mean? Let's just say he HAS A VERY SHINY NOSE.

And, as a matter of fact, if you ever saw it, YOU would even say it glows. It shines a brilliant, beautiful hue. It's true. This reindeer is uniquely Nova Scotian. You see, we've all heard about Rudolph, the Red-nosed Reindeer, but this little fellow is BUDDY, the BLUENOSE REINDEER!

Now, even though Buddy is a reindeer and his nose is an unusual colour,
he's altogether different from Rudolph.
But he is related. Buddy is
Rudolph's first cousin,
once removed, on his
mother's side. A typi-
cal Nova Scotian
family connection.
Though, if you
asked me the
classic Nova
Scotian question,
"What's his father's
name?"…I'm not sure I could answer.
I think it's Angus.

Anyway, Buddy the Bluenose Reindeer joined Santa's famous gang up at the North Pole. Now, I know what you're thinking. You're guessing that all of the other reindeer used to laugh and call him names. Am I right?

Nahhh! The other reindeer were fine with Buddy's blue schnozz. After all, they were used to differences in appearance, what with Rudolph's remarkable redness and all. They didn't judge. They liked Buddy and his nose and the story of his Nova Scotian past.

But I'm getting ahead of myself. Here's how Buddy came to join their team:

It was the eve of Christmas Eve, the day before the day before Christmas, to be exact, and Santa was getting frantic.

His guiding light, the trusty Rudolph, wasn't feeling well. He was sneezing and wheezing and sniffling and whiffling.

"Oh no!" thought Santa. Rudolph had a cold in his red nose. And it was a bad one, too. This was a Christmas crisis: Rudolph was going to be too under the weather to fly over the weather. With Christmas quickly approaching, how could Santa fly without his bright light to guide him through the sky?

Meanwhile, blue-nosed Buddy,
down in Nova Scotia, was having some
problems of his own. You see, this all
happened years ago, back in the age of
wooden sailing ships, and Buddy had
been adopted as a mascot on board a
Nova Scotian fishing schooner.

They say this little deer was from
Port Joli, which makes sense. But he
was having a very unjolly time fitting
in. Oh sure, the captain liked him.

Captain Nick was his name. Nick Klaus. From Lunenburg, he was. His wife, Clara Klaus, came from Christmas Island, Cape Breton. She was on board too and she really took a shining to Buddy's nose, so to speak.

The crew, however...well, that was another story. They were a bit jealous.

They didn't want Buddy on their ship. In fact, THEY used to laugh and call him names. And they never let poor Buddy play in their FUN DORY GAMES.

Out at sea, you see, the fishermen used to have a great time. They would jump in their wooden row-boats—called dories—and get lowered down the side of the ship. Once they were down, they would row out to their nets as fast as they could. It was a race! It was wonderful fun.

But Buddy, sweet Buddy, the Bluenose reindeer, wasn't allowed to play. Those crabby fishermen wouldn't let Buddy in a boat. Wouldn't allow him to get lowered down, to play in the rowing games. It was very sad.

Buddy was sorry he had no dory. The poor little deer was feeling rather…blue. As you might expect.

But, that all changed on this legendary eve of Christmas Eve. Well, actually it was a foggy, choppy, salt-sprayin', blowin'-a-gale, hurricane-force eve of Christmas Eve! The captain hadn't planned to be on the seas in such rough weather, but a nasty winter squall had roared up so fast that the ship and crew were caught unaware and unprepared.

The schooner lurched wildly on the waves, and the normally tough crew was starting to look scared. Under black clouds, the schooner was at risk of smashing against rocks hidden by the growing darkness of the storm. Captain Nick grabbed the wheel tighter and, squinting against the driving

drizzle, he desperately tried to steer his ship blindly through the storm. But it was hopeless. He could barely see.

Just then he caught sight of Buddy up by the mainmast, straining with the rest of the crew on the ropes. As Buddy looked back, he saw the captain carefully walking up the slippery wooden deck.

On that drizzly, foggy eve of Christmas Eve, the captain came to say:

"Buddy, with your nose so blue...won't you guide our schooner through?"

Sure enough, Buddy stepped forward on the slick, slanted deck. Rearing up, he fixed himself proudly in place at the bow of the bobbing schooner. He stuck his bright blue nose out over the bowsprit and lighted the schooner's way through the darkness, past the dangerous rocky shores where the waves were crashing.

Buddy stayed at his post until the vessel was guided right through the Atlantic storm and into calm waters. He saved the ship! And the crew too! Buddy came through the crisis with flying colours.

(And, just as an aside, THAT is why Nova Scotia's famous schooner is known to this day as "Bluenose"…because of that dear little deer, not afraid to stick his nose out when needed.)

Captain Nick and Clara Klaus
were thrilled and relieved that the ship
was rescued. The captain decided to
reward Buddy with a big surprise. He
would let the little deer join him in
the captain's very own rowboat:
Buddy was going to be lowered down
to join in the fishermen's rowing
races. Then, how the schooner crew

loved him! And they shouted out
with glee! They pointed to the captain
and shouted:

"Buddy the Bluenose Reindeer...
YOU'LL GO DOWN IN
HIS DOR-Y!"

Everyone on board cheered and clapped and celebrated.

Now, guess who was watching over this festive scene? It was that jolly old fellow who sees you when you're sleeping and knows when you're awake: Santa Claus! Santa was smiling because he knew that Buddy had been a good deer, good, for goodness' sake. And he saw the solution to his own nosey problem.

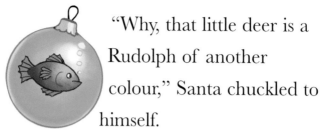 "Why, that little deer is a Rudolph of another colour," Santa chuckled to himself.

Later that night, just after finishing his last-minute Christmas preparations, Santa swooped down to Nova Scotia in his magical sleigh. He was going to make Buddy an offer he couldn't refuse. He wanted Buddy to become his best back-up reindeer: Rudolph's stand-in. Santa asked Buddy if he would be a replacement bulb to shine the way for his quickly approaching Christmas Eve flight. Buddy was overjoyed at the invitation! Filling in for the famous Rudolph? That's a reindeer's dream come true. He would be thrilled to lend his nose to Santa's cause.

So, with Captain Nick, Clara Klaus,
and the schoonermen all waving and
wishing him luck, the Bluenose reindeer
flew off with Santa in his sleigh, headed
for the North Pole. Considering all that
had happened, Buddy was glad for his
blue nose. He couldn't wait to join
Santa's team of reindeer.

But…he was just a little worried. He
could sail and he could row, but he was
pretty sure that he didn't know how to
fly. How exactly, he wondered to himself, was a simple schooner deer from

Nova Scotia going to take to the air with a team of magical flying reindeer on Christmas Eve? Buddy was puzzling that problem as the sleigh swooped down and slid to a stop.

Santa's workshop was busy, busy, busy. The elves were frantic with last-minute toy tinkering, and the other reindeer were carefully checking their harnesses for any last-minute fixes. For

the first time, Buddy could see the
other deer up close, all eight of them:
Dasher and Dancer and Prancer and
Vixen, Comet and Cupid, and
Donner and Blitzen. About as big as a
schooner crew, thought Buddy. And
that made Santa their skipper.
Captain Christmas!

Just then, Rudolph himself stepped forward. Buddy was nervous. What would Rudolph think of having a replacement deer of a different colour? Would his nose be out of joint? Rudolph sneezed. Then he snorted in the cold air and drew closer. The two deer came nose to nose, and Rudolph's red glow looked sickly and sore. Buddy's snout was shiny like a bright blue bulb on a Christmas tree. As the two bucks

shared their two cents' worth their noses formed a purplish halo of light.

"How's she goin', cousin?" said Rudolph. "What's goin' on?"

Buddy smiled a big smile. Rudolph was glad to see him. The two distant deer cousins laughed and got caught up on news from back home. He told Rudolph about his schooner adventures back in Nova Scotia, and Rudolph told Buddy exciting stories of pulling Santa's sleigh in Christmases past. The two shiny-nosed deer were brightly lighted and delighted.

The next day was the big day. It was a foggy Christmas Eve. And Santa came to say, "Rudolph with your nose so red, you better take an Aspirin and go to bed!"

Then Santa turned to say, "Buddy, with your nose so blue…"

"Yes, yes," said Buddy, "I'd LOVE to!"

His chance to light Santa's sleigh in Rudolph's place had finally come! The reindeer crew couldn't believe it. They wondered if young Buddy was really ready for such a big job. After all, how could they complete Santa's traditional Christmas Eve gift-giving journey

around the world with a rookie, substitute deer lighting the way? They just didn't think the idea would fly. And they knew for sure that Buddy couldn't. How would this work?

Buddy was certainly beginning to wonder what Santa had in mind.

The big magical red bag of presents was prepared. The long, long list was checked and checked again. Santa's red suit was pressed and ready. Then it was time to bring toys and joys to good girls and boys all over the world.

With a wink and whistle, Santa
Claus called to Buddy and the other
reindeer. He led them through the
snow, out behind his workshop.

"But...but...the sleigh is out front,"
said Buddy, feeling confused.

As Buddy and his buddies rounded
the corner, they looked up in amazement.
They couldn't believe what their eyes
were seeing. Santa Claus, with his big
red bag of toys, was standing high up
on the deck of a huge
wooden fishing
schooner.

"I borrowed this from my good friends Nick and Clara Klaus down in Nova Scotia," said Santa with a twinkle in his eye.

Something magical had happened to the ship—it was floating in the air, above the snow! And of course it had been painted a bright Christmas red. Thousands of tiny, sparkling lights flashed like fireflies all around the vessel. It was awesome!

"Ho, ho, heeeeave ho!" shouted
Santa, pointing down to the ropes that
kept the magic floating vessel
anchored to land. The reindeer
jumped to it. All hooves on deck!
They untied the schooner, and pulled
up the ropes. They each wiggled into
the sleigh harnesses that had been
lashed to the bow of the schooner.
And with that, Santa's reindeer leaped
for the sky. There was a powerful

"whoosh" sound as they lifted the big ship up, up into the air. Anchors aweigh!

The good ship *Christmas* sailed into the night with Santa at the helm. Up at the bow of the strange flying ship stood Buddy the Bluenose Reindeer. Like an oddly coloured lighthouse, the bright blue beacon on his snout lit up the darkness. The flying reindeer in front pulled the big schooner faster and faster through the starry sky. Swooshing down to rooftops, Santa went "ashore" from his sailing ship to deliver his Christmas cargo down the chimneys. He had gifts for all the kids of the right toy age for the voyage.

For Buddy, this trip was more fun than any dory race! All too soon, though, the night was nearly over. Santa had just one more house to visit.

Way out in the ocean is the Nova
Scotian island called Sable, which is just
a thin strip of land. Buddy knew it
from his sailing days. Only one family
lived on Sable Island, in a small house.
Wild horses ran by in herds, over snow-
covered sand dunes. The children
hoped and wished that Santa would

find them way out there. They weren't wishing for a pony that Christmas; they already had plenty. They were hoping for shiny new toys that made lots of noise. And new storybooks too. And candy.

Now, hang on to your hat. This is where the story gets even more exciting.

Santa's flying schooner swooped down toward the narrow little island. As the open sea came closer, Buddy could see from his perch at the bow

that a winter storm was swirling
below. Not again! he thought. But
this one was worse than any ocean
storm the sailor deer had ever seen.
Giant crashing waves smashed onto
the island's snowy beaches. The wind
blew in great blustery gusts. The
reindeer strained to keep their magic
flying ship upright. It was not a good
scene at all.

Onward the flying reindeer flew!
Dashing through the snow, they set
one course all the way. But the roof of
the island house was icy, and the
zooming schooner was moving too
fast. In the blink of an eye, it skipped
off the house and landed with a
splash out in the stormy ocean waves.

The freezing winter air made thick
ice form quickly all over the schooner.
The ship was too heavy now for the
reindeer to lift. Strong winds were
pushing the schooner sideways toward
the island's shore. They were going to
be shipwrecked on the beach!

Buddy had enough sailor sense to
know that something had to be done
right away. Santa wasn't used to sailing

a ship that couldn't fly, especially on a dark and stormy night. Buddy signalled the other reindeer to heave on the ropes. Up went the big white sails and they filled with wind in an instant.

The red schooner zoomed across the choppy water, heading straight for the shoreline. In the bright blue light

from Buddy's shiny nose, Santa could see the sand bar coming at them.

"Ho ho hooold on!" he called out, grasping tight to the ship's wheel. The reindeer braced themselves. Under full sail, at top speed, that Christmas schooner plowed head-on into the sandy strip of shore. With a great shudder, the ship pushed its way through to the open water on the other side.

They made it! Buddy saved the ship! The deer all cheered. Santa cheered too.

Phhhhew! That was close. When it comes to sailing in times of trouble, Buddy "nose" what to do.

Oh, and don't worry about the island kids. As the ship cut across that sandbar, Santa tossed their toys ashore in a big wooden captain's trunk. What a wonderful Christmas treasure they found in the sand when they woke up the next morning. X-mas marks the spot!

The ice melted away from the schooner, and with a "Ho ho hoooome!" Santa signalled his reindeer to fly.

Schwoosh!…the red schooner *Christmas* swept high into the night sky once again. It was headed on a course due north.

BUDDY

And this time, Buddy the Bluenose Reindeer would go down in HISTOR–Y.

❄ ❄ ❄

At least, that's the way I heard it.

It's a story Santa loved to tell, of a very Merry Christmas…

and a
Happy New Deer!